HUMAN HABITATS

BLOOD

By
Robin Twiddy

Enslow
PUBLISHING

Published in 2022 by Enslow Publishing, LLC
101 W. 23rd Street, Suite 240,
New York, NY 10011

Copyright © 2022 Booklife Publishing
This edition published by arrangement with Booklife Publishing

Cataloging-in-Publication Data

Names: Twiddy, Robin.
Title: Blood / Robin Twiddy.
Description: New York : Enslow Publishing, 2022. | Series: Human habitats | Includes glossary and index.
Identifiers: ISBN 9781978523449 (pbk.) | ISBN 9781978523463 (library bound) | ISBN 9781978523456 (6 pack) | ISBN 9781978523470 (ebook)
Subjects: LCSH: Blood--Juvenile literature. | Cardiovascular system--Juvenile literature. | Human physiology--Juvenile literature.
Classification: LCC QP91.T95 2022 | DDC 612.1'1--dc23

Designer: Gareth Liddington
Editor: John Wood

Printed in the United States of America

CPSIA compliance information: Batch #CS22ENS: For further information contact Enslow Publishing, New York, New York at 1-800-542-2595

TRICKY WORDS

Bacterium = singular
(one bacterium)
Bacteria = plural (many bacteria)
Bacterial = to do with a bacterium
or many bacteria

Fungus = singular (one fungus)
Fungi = plural (many fungi)
Fungal = to do with a fungus
or many fungi

Photo credits:

Cover - Anatolir, 4 - Puwadoi Jaturawutthichai, Fun Way Illustration, 6 - eveleen, 8 - AlZhi, LDarin, 12 - Roi and Roi.

Images are courtesy of Shutterstock.com. With thanks to Getty Images, Thinkstock Photo, and iStockphoto.

All facts, statistics, web addresses and URLs in this book were verified as valid and accurate at time of writing.
No responsibility for any changes to external websites or references can be accepted by either the author or publisher.

CONTENTS

Page 4   Welcome to the Human Habitat

Page 6   Life's Blood of the Human Habitat

Page 8   Red Rapids

Page 10   The Workers in the Blood

Page 12   Defenders of the Habitat

Page 14   Repairing a Hole

Page 16   Blood Fluke

Page 18   Sleeping Sickness

Page 20   Babesiosis

Page 22   It's a Gusher, Bye!

Page 24   Glossary and Index

Words that look like <u>this</u> can be found in the glossary on page 24.

WELCOME TO THE HUMAN HABITAT

Hi! I'm Mini Ventura. My cameraman, Dave, and I have been shrunk down so we can make a nature <u>documentary</u> all about the tiny things living in and on us. Follow us into the human <u>habitat</u> — a world within a world.

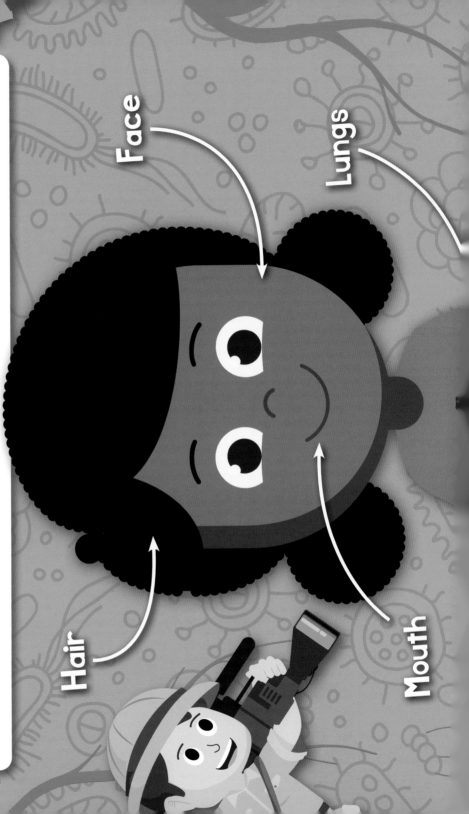

Face

Lungs

Hair

Mouth

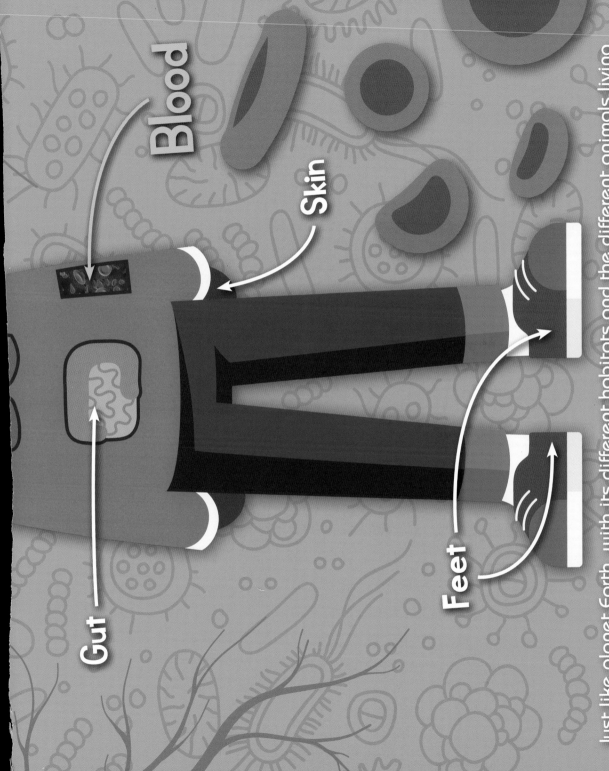

Blood

Skin

Gut

Feet

Just like planet Earth, with its different habitats and the different animals living in them, the human body has many different places that are home to lots of tiny living things. Today, we will be exploring the blood and just a few of the things living in it.

LIFE'S BLOOD OF THE HUMAN HABITAT

Deep in the heart of this habitat is the... ahem, heart. Blood flows to and from the heart and all around the human habitat.

The blood travels around the circulatory system and back to the heart.

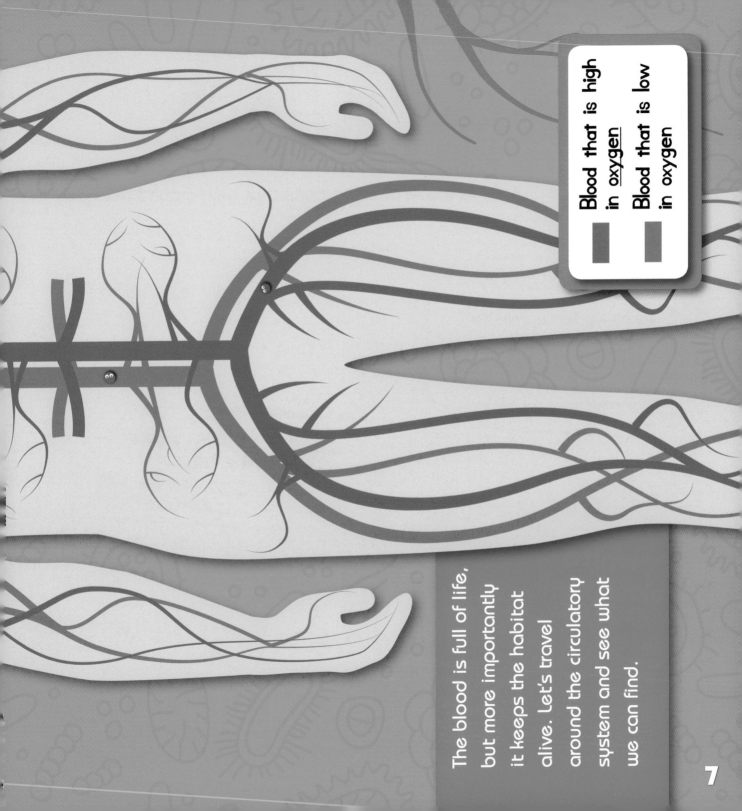

The blood is full of life, but more importantly it keeps the habitat alive. Let's travel around the circulatory system and see what we can find.

RED RAPIDS

Blood flows through the body at a speed of about 3 to 4 miles (4.8 to 6.4 km) per hour. That's fast! Blood is made of living parts that rush around the body doing important jobs.

It takes under a minute for blood to make it all the way around your body.

White blood cell

Platelet

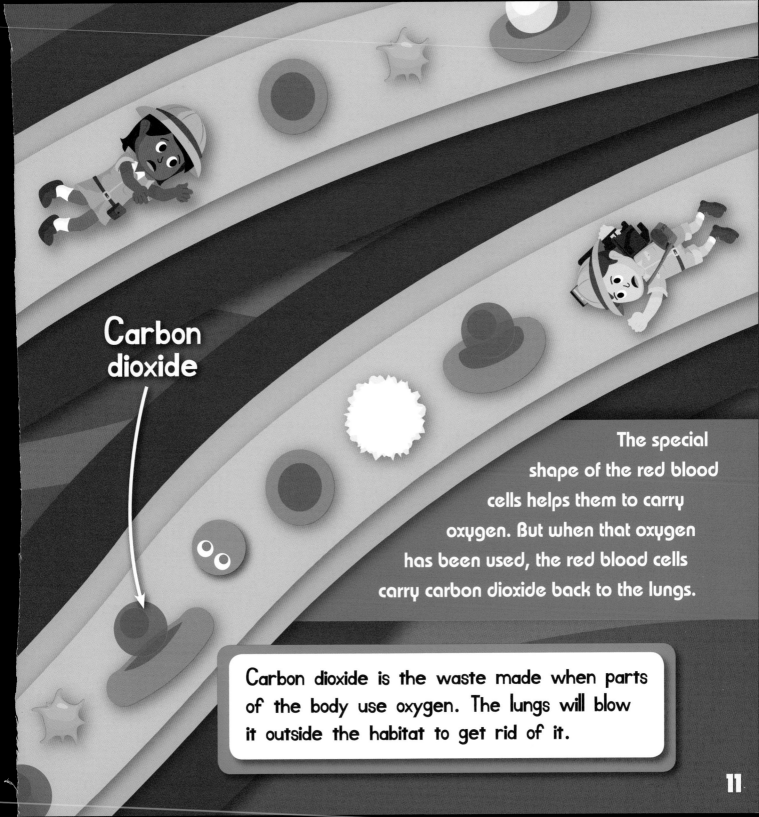

Carbon dioxide

The special shape of the red blood cells helps them to carry oxygen. But when that oxygen has been used, the red blood cells carry carbon dioxide back to the lungs.

Carbon dioxide is the waste made when parts of the body use oxygen. The lungs will blow it outside the habitat to get rid of it.

DEFENDERS OF THE HABITAT

These white blood cells travel all around the human habitat looking for <u>invaders</u>.

They are less common than the red blood cells, but these white blood cells are just as important. They are very territorial, which means they protect the area that they think of as their own.

The white blood cells seem very calm as they float around the bloodstream. However, don't be fooled — they are always ready for a fight!

Some white blood cells only live between one and three days. But the body is always making more.

REPAIRING A HOLE

Wow, this is the perfect chance to see the blood cells in action. Do you see that cut there? It is letting <u>bacteria</u> in. The blood cells will work together to fix it.

Cut

Platelet

Those white blood cells are tough. We will be in trouble if they mistake us for bacteria. I'm not hanging around.

See the platelets joining together? They're making a scab to cover the hole. This will stop red blood cells from getting out and bacteria from getting in.

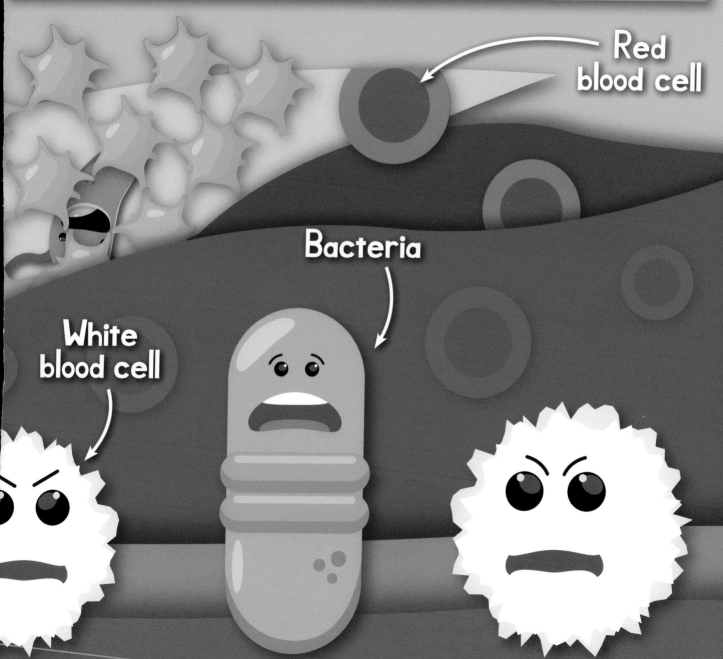

Red blood cell

Bacteria

White blood cell

BLOOD FLUKE

Well, we are really in luck today. That is a blood fluke over there. It is a type of <u>parasite</u> that lives in the blood vessels. It can lay between 300 and 3,000 eggs a day!

Blood fluke

These worms can live for up to 30 years. Watch how the white blood cells just swim right by it. We're not sure why, but the white blood cells don't seem to see them.

SLEEPING SICKNESS

Trypanosoma brucei

Oh, there are a lot of parasites in this human habitat. That worm is called *Trypanosoma brucei*. I know that's hard to say, but don't worry — there isn't a quiz! This parasite causes an illness called sleeping sickness.

Look! The sleeping sickness worms are <u>multiplying</u>. They will swim along in the bloodstream until they reach the brain habitat, and that is when they will cause the most damage.

I think we should get out of here before there are any more of them!

A little help?

BABESIOSIS

Look closely at the red blood cells as they pass by. Did you notice anything strange? Some of them seem to have something inside them.

This parasite gets into the bloodstream from the bite of a tick.

This looks like a nasty case of babesiosis. Some of the red blood cells have a parasite living in them. This is a pretty _rare_ parasite.

I might have to take one of these home for my collection.

IT'S A GUSHER, BYE!

There was a lot to see in the blood. There were lots of different blood cells doing their jobs and a surprising number of parasites!

GLOSSARY

bacteria	tiny living things, too small to see, that can cause diseases
cells	the basic building blocks of all living things
circulatory system	the veins, tubes, and organs in which the blood moves around in the body
documentary	a film that looks at real facts and events
habitat	the natural home in which animals, plants, and other living things live
invaders	a group of things that have entered a place that they are not from or welcome in
liquid	a material that flows, such as water
multiplying	becoming more and more in number
oxygen	a natural gas that many living things need in order to survive
parasite	a creature that lives on or in another creature
rare	uncommon and hard to find

INDEX

bacteria 14–15
blood flukes 16–17
brain 10, 19
cells 9–15, 17, 20–22
defend 12–13

oxygen 7, 10–11
parasites 16–22
platelets 8–9, 14–15, 23
repairing 14–15
worms 16–19

Inside the blood are platelets (we will see what they do later), white blood cells, and red blood cells. Each one of them has their own job in the habitat.

The liquid part of blood is called plasma. It is salty water with lots of things in it that are important for the habitat.

Red blood cell

THE WORKERS IN THE BLOOD

Oxygen

Inside the blood are the red blood cells. Look closely at them. They are carrying oxygen. The red blood cells are the workers of the human habitat. They carry important things around the body.

Oxygen is used all around the human habitat to help power things such as the brain.